GREATEST
ever AESOP'S
FABLES

Gayatri Kalra Sehgal is an internationally acclaimed author, an artist and a passionate educationist. She set up a daycare centre and two schools, first as the principal and later as a dean, and carefully designed their academic curricula. In 2013, she innovated and revolutionized a novel way of writing report cards, renaming them as 'Child's Intelligence Profile'.

She regularly conducts interactive seminars and engaging workshops on the National Education Policy 2020 (NEP 2020), child development, learning styles, curriculum design, effective communication, authorpreneurship, emotional well-being during the pandemic, and more, sensitizing educators towards holistic teaching and learning approaches. Her work, including her motivational speeches, is aimed at encouraging awareness and sensitivity, and offering support to parents of differently-abled children.

Her 13 published books are an extensive collection of her unique experiences and her vision to inspire global leaders for tomorrow.

Also by the Author

Tales of Fairies, Witches and Magic
Stories of Dragons and Beasts
Become a Mathematician in 21 Days
Become a Brilliant Thinker in 21 Days
Become a Creative Genius in 21 Days
Being a Mathematician: Mastering Secrets of Mental Math
Being a Brilliant Thinker: Mastering Intelligent Thinking Skills
Being a Creative Genius: Mastering Activities That Inspire Creativity
Super Child! Unlocking the Secrets of Working Memory
Winning Strategies for Parents: Helping Your Child Excel at Home and School

GREATEST *ever* AESOP'S FABLES

Gayatri Kalra Sehgal

Published by
Rupa Publications India Pvt. Ltd 2023
7/16, Ansari Road, Daryaganj
New Delhi 110002

Sales centres:
Bengaluru Chennai
Hyderabad Jaipur Kathmandu
Kolkata Mumbai Prayagraj

Edition copyright © Rupa Publications India Pvt. Ltd 2023

All rights reserved.
No part of this publication may be reproduced, transmitted,
or stored in a retrieval system, in any form or by any means,
electronic, mechanical, photocopying, recording or otherwise,
without the prior permission of the publisher.

P-ISBN: 978-93-5702-869-1
E-ISBN: 978-93-5702-968-1

First impression 2023

10 9 8 7 6 5 4 3 2 1

Printed in India

This book is sold subject to the condition that it shall not,
by way of trade or otherwise, be lent, resold, hired out, or otherwise
circulated, without the publisher's prior consent, in any form of
binding or cover other than that in which it is published.

To my sons,
Divyamshu and Kuber

Contents

Fable 1	The Ants and the Grasshopper	1
Fable 2	The Lion and the Mouse	3
Fable 3	The Hare and the Tortoise	5
Fable 4	The Ass and Its Shadow	6
Fable 5	The Town Mouse and the Country Mouse	8
Fable 6	The Fox and the Goat	10
Fable 7	The Goose and the Golden Egg	12
Fable 8	The Crow and the Pitcher	14
Fable 9	The Vain Jackdaw and His Borrowed Feathers	15
Fable 10	The Heron	17
Fable 11	The Lion, the Fox and the Ass	19
Fable 12	The Ant and the Dove	21
Fable 13	The Mice and the Weasels	22
Fable 14	The Two Pots	24
Fable 15	The Charcoal-Burner and the Fuller	26
Fable 16	The North Wind and the Sun	27

Fable 17	The Mole and His Mother	28
Fable 18	The Lion, the Mouse and the Fox	29
Fable 19	The Lark and Her Young Ones	30
Fable 20	The Crab and Its Mother	32
Fable 21	The Goatherd and the Wild Goats	33
Fable 22	The Shepherd's Boy and the Wolf	35
Fable 23	The Miller, His Son and the Ass	36
Fable 24	The Fox Without a Tail	39
Fable 25	The Fox and the Crow	41
Fable 26	The Wolf and the Sheep	43
Fable 27	Belling the Cat	44
Fable 28	The Man and His Two Sweethearts	46
Fable 29	The Eagle and the Jackdaw	47
Fable 30	The Bowman and Lion	49
Fable 31	Hercules and the Wagoner	50
Fable 32	The Mouse, the Frog and the Hawk	52
Fable 33	The Fox and the Grapes	54
Fable 34	The Animals and the Plague	56
Fable 35	The Bundle of Sticks	58
Fable 36	The Fir-Tree and the Bramble	60
Fable 37	A Raven and a Swan	61
Fable 38	The Dog and His Reflection	62
Fable 39	The Lioness	63
Fable 40	The Astrologer	64
Fable 41	The Thief and the Innkeeper	66
Fable 42	The Ass and the Lap Dog	68
Fable 43	The Milkmaid and Her Pail	70
Fable 44	The Huntsman and the Fisherman	72

Fable 45	The Gnat and the Bull	73
Fable 46	The Miser	74
Fable 47	The Cat, the Cock and the Young Mouse	76
Fable 48	The Monkey and the Dolphin	78
Fable 49	The Cock and the Fox	80
Fable 50	The Old Woman and the Wine-Jar	82
Fable 51	The Stag at the Pool	83

Acknowledgements   85

Fable 1

The Ants and the Grasshopper

One bright day in late autumn a family of Ants was bustling about in the warm sunshine, drying out the grain they had stored up during the summer, when a starving Grasshopper, his fiddle under his arm, came up and humbly begged for a bite to eat.

'What!' cried the Ants in surprise, 'haven't you stored anything away for the winter? What in the world were you doing all last summer?'

'I didn't have time to store up any food,' whined the Grasshopper; 'I was so busy making music that before I knew it the summer was gone.'

The Ants shrugged their shoulders in disgust.

'Making music, were you?' they cried. 'Very well; now dance!' And they turned their backs on the Grasshopper and went on with their work.

There's a time for work and a time for play.

Fable 2

The Lion and the Mouse

A Lion lay asleep in the forest, his great head resting on his paws. A timid little Mouse came upon him unexpectedly, and in her fright and haste to get away, ran across the Lion's nose. Roused from his nap, the Lion laid his huge paw angrily on the tiny creature to kill her.

'Spare me!' begged the poor Mouse. 'Please let me go and some day I will surely repay you.'

The Lion was much amused to think that a Mouse could ever help him. But he was generous and finally let the Mouse go.

Some days later, while stalking his prey in the forest, the Lion was caught in the toils of a hunter's net. Unable to free himself, he filled the forest with his angry roaring. The Mouse knew the voice and quickly found the Lion struggling in the net. Running to one of the great ropes that bound him, she gnawed it until it parted, and soon the Lion was free.

'You laughed when I said I would repay you,' said the Mouse. 'Now you see that even a Mouse can help a Lion.'

A kindness is never wasted.

Fable 3

The Hare and the Tortoise

A Hare one day ridiculed the short feet and slow pace of the Tortoise, who replied, laughing: 'Though you be swift as the wind, I will beat you in a race.' The Hare, believing her assertion to be simply impossible, assented to the proposal; and they agreed that the Fox should choose the course and fix the goal. On the day appointed for the race the two started together. The Tortoise never for a moment stopped, but went on with a slow but steady pace straight to the end of the course. The Hare, lying down by the wayside, fell fast asleep. At last waking up, and moving as fast as he could, he saw the Tortoise had already reached the goal, and was comfortably dozing after her fatigue.

Slow but steady wins the race.

Fable 4

The Ass and Its Shadow

A Traveller had hired an Ass to carry him to a distant part of the country. The owner of the Ass went with the Traveller, walking beside him to drive the Ass and point out the way.

The road led across a treeless plain where the Sun beat down fiercely. So intense did the heat become that the Traveller at last decided to stop for a rest, and as there was no other shade to be found, the Traveller sat down in the shadow of the Ass.

Now the heat had affected the Driver as much as it had the Traveller, and even more, for he had been walking. Wishing also to rest in the shade cast by the Ass, he began to quarrel with the Traveller, saying he had hired the Ass and not the shadow it cast.

The Ass and Its Shadow
The two soon came to blows, and while they were fighting, the Ass took to its heels.

In quarreling about the shadow we often lose the substance.

Fable 5

The Town Mouse and the Country Mouse

A Town Mouse once visited a relative who lived in the country. For lunch the Country Mouse served wheat stalks, roots and acorns, with a dash of cold water for drink. The Town Mouse ate very sparingly, nibbling a little of this and a little of that, and by her manner making it very plain that she ate the simple food only to be polite.

After the meal the friends had a long talk, or rather the Town Mouse talked about her life in the city while the Country Mouse listened. They then went to bed in a cozy nest in the hedgerow and slept in quiet and comfort until morning.

In her sleep the Country Mouse dreamed she was a Town Mouse The Town Mouse and The Country Mouse with all

The Town Mouse and the Country Mouse

the luxuries and delights of city life that her friend had described for her. So the next day when the Town Mouse asked the Country Mouse to go home with her to the city, she gladly said yes.

When they reached the mansion in which the Town Mouse lived, they found on the table in the dining room the leavings of a very fine banquet. There were sweetmeats and jellies, pastries, delicious cheeses, indeed, the most tempting foods that a Mouse can imagine. But just as the Country Mouse was about to nibble a dainty bit of pastry, she heard a Cat mew loudly and scratch at the door.

In great fear the Mice scurried to a hiding place, where they lay quite still for a long time, hardly daring to breathe. When at last they ventured back to the feast, the door opened suddenly and in came the servants to clear the table, followed by the House Dog.

The Country Mouse stopped in the Town Mouse's den only long enough to pick up her carpet bag and umbrella.

'You may have luxuries and dainties that I have not,' she said as she hurried away, 'but I prefer my plain food and simple life in the country with the peace and security that go with it.'

Poverty with security is better than plenty in the midst of fear and uncertainty.

Fable 6

The Fox and the Goat

A Fox fell into a well, and though it was not very deep, he found that he could not get out. After he had been in the well a long time, a thirsty Goat came by.

The Goat thought the Fox had gone down to drink, and so he asked if the water was good.

'The finest in the whole country,' said the crafty Fox, 'jump in and try it. There is more than enough for both of us.'

The thirsty Goat immediately jumped in and began to drink. The Fox just as quickly jumped on the Goat's back and leaped from the tip of the Goat's horns out of the well.

The foolish Goat now saw what a plight he had got into, and begged the Fox to help him out. But the Fox was already on his way to the woods.

The Fox and the Goat

'If you had as much sense as you have beard, old fellow,' he said as he ran, 'you would have been more cautious about finding a way to get out again before you jumped in.'

Look before you leap.

Fable 7

The Goose and the Golden Egg

There was once a Countryman who possessed the most wonderful Goose you can imagine, for every day when he visited the nest, the Goose had laid a beautiful, glittering, golden egg.

The Countryman took the eggs to market and soon began to get rich. But it was not long before he grew impatient with the Goose because she gave him only a single golden egg a day. He was not getting rich fast enough.

Then one day, after he had finished counting his money, the idea came to him that he could get all the golden eggs at once by killing the Goose and cutting it open. But when the deed

The Goose and the Golden Egg

The Goose and The Golden Egg was done, not a single golden egg did he find, and his precious Goose was dead.

*__Those who have plenty want more
and so lose all they have.__*

Fable 8

The Crow and the Pitcher

In a spell of dry weather, when the Birds could find very little to drink, a thirsty Crow found a pitcher with a little water in it. But the pitcher was high and had a narrow neck, and no matter how he tried, the Crow could not reach the water. The poor thing felt as if he must die of thirst.

Then an idea came to him. Picking up some small pebbles, he dropped them into the pitcher one by one. With each pebble the water rose a little higher until at last it was near enough so he could drink.

In a pinch a good use of our wits may help us out.

Fable 9

The Vain Jackdaw and His Borrowed Feathers

A Jackdaw chanced to fly over the garden of the King's palace. There he saw with much wonder and envy a flock of royal Peacocks in all the glory of their splendid plumage.

Now the black Jackdaw was not a very handsome bird, nor very refined in manner. Yet he imagined that all he needed to make himself fit for the society of the Peacocks was a dress like theirs. So he picked up some cast-off feathers of the Peacocks and stuck them among his own black plumes.

Dressed in his borrowed finery he strutted loftily among the birds of his own kind. Then he flew down into the garden among the Peacocks. But they soon saw who he was. Angry at the cheat, they flew at him, plucking away the borrowed feathers and also some of his own.

The poor Jackdaw returned sadly to his former companions. There another unpleasant surprise awaited him. They had not forgotten his superior airs towards them, and, to punish him, they drove him away with a rain of pecks and jeers.

Borrowed feathers do not make fine birds.

Fable 10

The Heron

A Heron was walking sedately along the bank of a stream, his eyes on the clear water, and his long neck and pointed bill ready to snap up a likely morsel for his breakfast. The clear water swarmed with fish, but Master Heron was hard to please that morning.

'No small fry for me,' he said. 'Such scanty fare is not fit for a Heron.'

Now a fine young Perch swam near.

'No indeed,' said the Heron. 'I wouldn't even trouble to open my beak for anything like that!'

As the sun rose, the fish left the shallow water near the shore and swam below into the cool depths towards the middle. The Heron saw no more fish, and very glad was he at last to breakfast on a tiny Snail.

Do not be too hard to suit or you may have to be content with the worst or with nothing at all.

Fable 11

The Lion, the Fox and the Ass

The Lion, the Fox and the Ass entered into an agreement to assist each other in a chase. Having secured a large booty, the Lion on their return from the forest asked the Ass to allot the due portion to each of the three partners in the treaty.

The Ass carefully divided the spoil into three equal shares and modestly requested the two others to make the first choice.

The Lion, bursting out into a great rage, devoured the Ass. Then he requested the Fox to do him the favour to make a division.

The Fox accumulated all that they had killed into one large heap and left to himself the smallest possible morsel.

The Lion said, 'Who has taught you, my very excellent fellow, the art of division? You are perfect to a fraction.'

He replied, 'I learned it from the Ass, by witnessing his fate.'

*Happy is the man who learns
from the misfortunes of others.*

Fable 12

The Ant and the Dove

A Dove saw an Ant fall into a brook. The Ant struggled in vain to reach the bank, and in pity, the Dove dropped a blade of straw close beside it. Clinging to the straw like a shipwrecked sailor to a broken spar, the Ant floated safely to shore.

Soon after, the Ant saw a man getting ready to kill the Dove with a stone. But just as he cast the stone, the Ant stung him in the heel, so that the pain made him miss his aim, and the startled Dove flew to safety in a distant wood.

A kindness is never wasted.

Fable 13

The Mice and the Weasels

The Weasels and the Mice waged a perpetual war with each other, in which much blood was shed. The Weasels were always the victors.

The Mice thought that the cause of their frequent defeats was that they had no leaders set apart from the general army to command them, and that they were exposed to dangers from lack of discipline. They therefore chose as leaders Mice that were most renowned for their family descent, strength and counsel, as well as those most noted for their courage in the fight, so that they might be better marshaled in battle array and formed into troops, regiments, and battalions.

When all this was done, and the army disciplined, and the herald Mouse had duly proclaimed war by challenging the Weasels, the newly chosen generals bound their

The Mice and the Weasels

The Mice and the Weasels heads with straws, that they might be more conspicuous to all their troops.

Scarcely had the battle begun, when a great rout overwhelmed the Mice, who scampered off as fast as they could to their holes. The generals, not being able to get in on account of the ornaments on their heads, were all captured and eaten by the Weasels.

The more honour the more danger.

Fable 14

The Two Pots

Two Pots, one of brass and the other of clay, stood together on the hearthstone. One day the Brass Pot proposed to the Earthen Pot that they go out into the world together. But the Earthen Pot excused himself, saying that it would be wiser for him to stay in the corner by the fire.

'It would take so little to break me,' he said. 'You know how fragile I am. The least shock is sure to shatter me!"

'Don't let that keep you at home,' urged the Brass Pot. 'I shall take very good care of you. If we should happen to meet anything hard I will step between and save you.'

So the Earthen Pot at last consented, and the two set out side by side, jolting along on three stubby legs first to this side, then to that, and bumping into each other at every step.

The Earthen Pot could not survive that sort of

companionship very long. They had not gone ten paces before the Earthen Pot cracked, and at the next jolt he flew into a thousand pieces.

Equals make the best friends.

Fable 15

The Charcoal-Burner and the Fuller

A Charcoal-Burner carried on his trade in his own house. One day he met a friend, a Fuller, and entreated him to come and live with him, saying that they should be far better neighbours and that their housekeeping expenses would be lessened. The Fuller replied, 'The arrangement is impossible as far as I am concerned, for whatever I should whiten, you would immediately blacken again with your charcoal.'

Like will draw like.

Fable 16

The North Wind and the Sun

The North Wind and the Sun disputed as to which was the most powerful, and agreed that he should be declared the victor who could first strip a wayfaring man of his clothes.

The North Wind first tried his power and blew with all his might, but the keener his blasts, the closer the Traveller wrapped his cloak around him, until at last, resigning all hope of victory, the Wind called upon the Sun to see what he could do.

The Sun suddenly shone out with all his warmth. The Traveller no sooner felt his genial rays than he took off one garment after another, and at last, fairly overcome with heat, undressed and bathed in a stream that lay in his path.

Persuasion is better than force.

Fable 17

The Mole and His Mother

A little Mole once said to his Mother:
'Why, Mother, you said I was blind! But I am sure I can see!'

Mother Mole saw she would have to get such conceit out of his head. So she put a bit of frankincense before him and asked him to tell what it was.

The little Mole peered at it. 'Why, that's a pebble!'

'Well, my son, that proves you've lost your sense of smell along with still being blind.'

Boast of one thing and you will be found lacking in that and a few other things as well.

Fable 18

The Lion, the Mouse and the Fox

A Lion, fatigued by the heat of a summer's day, fell fast asleep in his den. A Mouse ran over his mane and ears and woke him from his slumbers. He rose up and shook himself in great wrath, and searched every corner of his den to find the Mouse. A Fox seeing him said: 'A fine Lion you are, to be frightened of a Mouse.' 'Tis not the Mouse I fear,' said the Lion; 'I resent his familiarity and ill-breeding.'

Little liberties are great offenses.

Fable 19

The Lark and Her Young Ones

A Lark made her nest in a field of young wheat. As the days passed, the wheat stalks grew tall and the young birds, too, grew in strength. Then one day, when the ripe golden grain waved in the breeze, the Farmer and his son came into the field.

'This wheat is now ready for reaping,' said the Farmer. 'We must call in our neighbours and friends to help us harvest it.'

The young Larks in their nest close by were much frightened, for they knew they would be in great danger if they did not leave the nest before the reapers came. When the Mother Lark returned with food for them, they told her what they had heard.

'Do not be frightened, children,' said the Mother Lark. 'If the Farmer said he would call in his neighbours and friends to help him do his work, this wheat will not be reaped for a while yet.'

A few days later, the wheat was so ripe, that when the wind shook the stalks, a hail of wheat grains came rustling down on the young Larks' heads.

'If this wheat is not harvested at once,' said the Farmer, 'we shall lose half the crop. We cannot wait any longer for help from our friends. Tomorrow we must set to work ourselves.'

When the young Larks told their mother what they had heard that day, she said:

'Then we must be off at once. When a man decides to do his own work and not depend on any one else, then you may be sure there will be no more delay.'

There was much fluttering and trying out of wings that afternoon, and at sunrise next day, when the Farmer and his son cut down the grain, they found an empty nest.

Self-help is the best help.

Fable 20
The Crab and Its Mother

A Crab said to her son, 'Why do you walk so one-sided, my child? It is far more becoming to go straight forward.' The young Crab replied: 'Quite true, dear Mother; and if you will show me the straight way, I will promise to walk in it.' The Mother tried in vain, and submitted without protest to the reproof of her child.

Example is more powerful than precept.

Fable 21

The Goatherd and the Wild Goats

A Goatherd, driving his flock from their pasture at eventide, found some Wild Goats mingled among them, and shut them up together with his own for the night.

The next day it snowed very hard, so that he could not take the herd to their usual feeding places, but was obliged to keep them in the fold. He gave his own goats just sufficient food to keep them alive, but fed the strangers more abundantly in the hope of enticing them to stay with him and of making them his own.

When the thaw set in, he led them all out to feed, and the Wild Goats scampered away as fast as they could to the mountains. The Goatherd scolded them for their ingratitude in leaving him, when during the storm he had taken more care of them than of his own herd.

One of them, turning about, said to him: 'That is the very reason why we are so cautious; for if you yesterday treated us better than the Goats you have had so long, it is plain also that if others came after us, you would in the same manner prefer them to ourselves.'

**Old friends cannot with impunity
be sacrificed for new ones.**

Fable 22

The Shepherd's Boy and the Wolf

A Shepherd-Boy, who watched a flock of sheep near a village, brought out the villagers three or four times by crying out, 'Wolf! Wolf!' and when his neighbours came to help him, laughed at them for their pains.

The Wolf, however, did truly come at last.

The Shepherd-boy, now really alarmed, shouted in an agony of terror: 'Pray, do come and help me; the Wolf is killing the sheep;' but no one paid any heed to his cries, nor rendered any assistance. The Wolf, having no cause of fear, at his leisure lacerated or destroyed the whole flock.

There is no believing a liar,
even when he speaks the truth.

Fable 23

The Miller, His Son and the Ass

One day, a long time ago, an old Miller and his Son were on their way to the market with an Ass which they hoped to sell. They drove him very slowly, for they thought they would have a better chance to sell him if they kept him in good condition. As they walked along the highway some travellers laughed loudly at them.

'What foolishness,' cried one, 'to walk when they might as well ride. The most stupid of the three is not the one you would expect it to be.'

The Miller did not like to be laughed at, so he told his son to climb up and ride.

They had gone a little farther along the road, when three merchants passed by.

'Oho, what have we here?' they cried. 'Respect old age,

The Miller, His Son and the Ass

young man! Get down, and let the old man ride.'

Though the Miller was not tired, he made the boy get down and climbed up himself to ride, just to please the Merchants.

At the next turnstile they overtook some women carrying market baskets loaded with vegetables and other things to sell.

'Look at the old fool,' exclaimed one of them. 'Perched on the Ass, while that poor boy has to walk.'

The Miller felt a bit vexed, but to be agreeable he told the Boy to climb up behind him.

They had no sooner started out again than a loud shout went up from another company of people on the road.

'What a crime,' cried one, 'to load up a poor dumb beast like that! They look more able to carry the poor creature, than he to carry them.'

'They must be on their way to sell the poor thing's hide,' said another.

The Miller and his Son quickly scrambled down, and a short time later, the market place was thrown into an uproar as the two came along carrying the Donkey slung from a pole. A great crowd of people ran out to get a closer look at the strange sight.

The Ass did not dislike being carried, but so many people came up to point at him and laugh and shout, that he began to kick and bray, and then, just as they were crossing a bridge, the ropes that held him gave way, and down he tumbled into the river.

The poor Miller now set out sadly for home. By trying

to please everybody, he had pleased nobody, and lost his Ass besides.

If you try to please all, you please none.

Fable 24

The Fox Without a Tail

A Fox that had been caught in a trap, succeeded at last, after much painful tugging, in getting away. But he had to leave his beautiful bushy tail behind him.

For a long time he kept away from the other Foxes, for he knew well enough that they would all make fun of him and crack jokes and laugh behind his back. But it was hard for him to live alone, and at last he thought of a plan that would perhaps help him out of his trouble.

He called a meeting of all the Foxes, saying that he had something of great importance to tell the tribe.

When they were all gathered together, the Fox Without a Tail got up and made a long speech about those Foxes who had come to harm because of their tails.

This one had been caught by hounds when his tail had

become entangled in the hedge. That one had not been able to run fast enough because of the weight of his brush. Besides, it was well known, he said, that men hunt Foxes simply for their tails, which they cut off as prizes of the hunt. With such proof of the danger and uselessness of having a tail, said Master Fox, he would advise every Fox to cut it off, if he valued life and safety.

When he had finished talking, an old Fox arose, and said, smiling:

'Master Fox, kindly turn around for a moment, and you shall have your answer.'

When the poor Fox Without a Tail turned around, there arose such a storm of jeers and hooting, that he saw how useless it was to try any longer to persuade the Foxes to part with their tails.

***Do not listen to the advice of him
who seeks to lower you to his own level.***

Fable 25

The Fox and the Crow

One bright morning as the Fox was following his sharp nose through the wood in search of a bite to eat, he saw a Crow on the limb of a tree overhead. This was by no means the first Crow the Fox had ever seen. What caught his attention this time and made him stop for a second look, was that the lucky Crow held a bit of cheese in her beak.

'No need to search any farther,' thought sly Master Fox. 'Here is a dainty bite for my breakfast.'

Up he trotted to the foot of the tree in which the Crow was sitting, and looking up admiringly, he cried, 'Good-morning, beautiful creature!'

The Crow, her head cocked on one side, watched the Fox suspiciously. But she kept her beak tightly closed on the cheese and did not return his greeting.

'What a charming creature she is!' said the Fox. 'How her feathers shine! What a beautiful form and what splendid wings! Such a wonderful Bird should have a very lovely voice, since everything else about her is so perfect. Could she sing just one song, I know I should hail her Queen of Birds.'

Listening to these flattering words, the Crow forgot all her suspicion, and also her breakfast. She wanted very much to be called Queen of Birds.

So she opened her beak wide to utter her loudest caw, and down fell the cheese straight into the Fox's open mouth.

'Thank you,' said Master Fox sweetly, as he walked off. 'Though it is cracked, you have a voice sure enough. But where are your wits?"

The flatterer lives at the expense of those who will listen to him.

Fable 26

The Wolf and the Sheep

A Wolf, sorely wounded and bitten by dogs, lay sick and maimed in his lair. Being in want of food, he called to a Sheep who was passing, and asked him to fetch some water from a stream flowing close beside him. 'For,' he said, 'if you will bring me drink, I will find means to provide myself with meat.'

'Yes,' said the Sheep, 'if I should bring you the draught, you would doubtless make me provide the meat also.'

Hypocritical speeches are easily seen through.

Fable 27

Belling the Cat

The Mice once called a meeting to decide on a plan to free themselves of their enemy, the Cat. At least they wished to find some way of knowing when she was coming, so they might have time to run away. Indeed, something had to be done, for they lived in such constant fear of her claws that they hardly dared stir from their dens by night or day.

Many plans were discussed, but none of them was thought good enough. At last a very young Mouse got up and said:

'I have a plan that seems very simple, but I know it will be successful. All we have to do is to hang a bell about the Cat's neck. When we hear the bell ringing we will know immediately that our enemy is coming.'

All the Mice were much surprised that they had not thought of such a plan before. But in the midst of the rejoicing

Belling the Cat

over their good fortune, an old Mouse arose and said:

'I will say that the plan of the young Mouse is very good. But let me ask one question, who will bell the Cat?"

It is one thing to say that something should be done, but quite a different matter to do it.

Fable 28

The Man and His Two Sweethearts

A Middle-Aged Man, whose hair had begun to turn grey, courted two women at the same time. One of them was young, and the other well advanced in years. The elder woman, ashamed to be courted by a man younger than herself, made a point, whenever her admirer visited her, to pull out some portion of his black hairs. The younger, on the contrary, not wishing to become the wife of an old man, was equally zealous in removing every grey hair she could find. Thus it came to pass that between them both he very soon found that he had not a hair left on his head.

Those who seek to please everybody please nobody.

Fable 29

The Eagle and the Jackdaw

An Eagle, swooping down on powerful wings, seized a lamb in her talons and made off with it to her nest. A Jackdaw saw the deed, and his silly head was filled with the idea that he was big and strong enough to do as the Eagle had done. So with much rustling of feathers and a fierce air, he came down swiftly on the back of a large Ram. But when he tried to rise again he found that he could not get away, for his claws were tangled in the wool. And so far was he from carrying away the Ram, that the Ram hardly noticed he was there.

The Shepherd saw the fluttering Jackdaw and at once guessed what had happened. Running up, he caught the bird and clipped its wings. That evening he gave the Jackdaw to his children.

'What a funny bird this is!' they said laughing, 'what do you call it, father?"

'That is a Jackdaw, my children. But if you should ask him, *he* would say he is an Eagle.'

> ***Do not let your vanity make you overestimate your powers.***

Fable 30

The Bowman and Lion

A very skillful Bowman went to the mountains in search of game, but all the beasts of the forest fled at his approach. The Lion alone challenged him to combat.

The Bowman immediately shot out an arrow and said to the Lion: 'I send thee my messenger, that from him thou mayest learn what I myself shall be when I assail thee.'

The wounded Lion rushed away in great fear, and when a Fox who had seen it all happen told him to be of good courage and not to back off at the first attack he replied: 'You counsel me in vain; for if he sends so fearful a messenger, how shall I abide the attack of the man himself?"

*Be on guard against men who
can strike from a distance.*

Fable 31

Hercules and the Wagoner

A Farmer was driving his wagon along a miry country road after a heavy rain. The horses could hardly drag the load through the deep mud, and at last came to a standstill when one of the wheels sank to the hub in a rut.

The farmer climbed down from his seat and stood beside the wagon looking at it but without making the least effort to get it out of the rut. All he did was to curse his bad luck and call loudly on Hercules to come to his aid.

Then, it is said, Hercules really did appear, saying:

'Put your shoulder to the wheel, man, and urge on your horses. Do you think you can move the wagon by simply looking at it and whining about it? Hercules will not help unless you make some effort to help yourself.'

And when the farmer put his shoulder to the wheel and

urged on the horses, the wagon moved very readily, and soon the Farmer was riding along in great content and with a good lesson learned.

Heaven helps those who help themselves.

Fable 32

The Mouse, the Frog and the Hawk

A Mouse who always lived on the land, by an unlucky chance formed an intimate acquaintance with a Frog, who lived for the most part in the water.

The Frog, one day intent on mischief, bound the foot of the Mouse tightly to his own. Thus joined together, the Frog first of all led his friend the Mouse to the meadow where they were accustomed to finding their food. After this, he gradually led him towards the pool in which he lived, until reaching the very brink, he suddenly jumped in, dragging the Mouse with him.

The Frog enjoyed the water amazingly, and swam croaking about, as if he had done a good deed. The unhappy Mouse was soon suffocated by the water, and his dead body floated about on the surface, tied to the foot of the Frog.

The Mouse, the Frog and the Hawk

A Hawk observed it, and, pouncing upon it with his talons, carried it aloft. The Frog, being still fastened to the leg of the Mouse, was also carried off a prisoner, and was eaten by the Hawk.

Harm hatch, harm catch.

Fable 33

The Fox and the Grapes

A Fox one day spied a beautiful bunch of ripe grapes hanging from a vine trained along the branches of a tree. The grapes seemed ready to burst with juice, and the Fox's mouth watered as he gazed longingly at them.

The bunch hung from a high branch, and the Fox had to jump for it. The first time he jumped he missed it by a long way. So he walked off a short distance and took a running leap at it, only to fall short once more. Again and again he tried, but in vain.

Now he sat down and looked at the grapes in disgust.

'What a fool I am,' he said. 'Here I am wearing myself out to get a bunch of sour grapes that are not worth gaping for.'

And off he walked very, very scornfully.

The Fox and the Grapes

There are many who pretend to despise and belittle that which is beyond their reach.

Fable 34

The Animals and the Plague

Once upon a time a severe plague raged among the animals. Many died, and those who lived were so ill, that they cared for neither food nor drink, and dragged themselves about listlessly. No longer could a fat young hen tempt Master Fox to dinner, nor a tender lamb rouse greedy Sir Wolf's appetite.

At last the Lion decided to call a council. When all the animals were gathered together he arose and said:

'Dear friends, I believe the gods have sent this plague upon us as a punishment for our sins. Therefore, the most guilty one of us must be offered in sacrifice. Perhaps we may thus obtain forgiveness and cure for all.

'I will confess all *my* sins first. I admit that I have been very greedy and have devoured many sheep. They had done me no harm. I have eaten goats and bulls and stags. To tell

The Animals and the Plague

the truth, I even ate up a shepherd now and then.

'Now, if I am the most guilty, I am ready to be sacrificed. But I think it best that each one confess his sins as I have done. Then we can decide in all justice who is the most guilty.'

'Your majesty,' said the Fox, 'you are too good. Can it be a crime to eat sheep, such stupid mutton heads? No, no, your majesty. You have done them great honour by eating them up.

'And so far as shepherds are concerned, we all know they belong to that puny race that pretends to be our masters.'

All the animals applauded the Fox loudly. Then, though the Tiger, the Bear, the Wolf, and all the savage beasts recited the most wicked deeds, all were excused and made to appear very saint-like and innocent.

It was now the Ass's turn to confess.

'I remember,' he said guiltily, 'that one day as I was passing a field belonging to some priests, I was so tempted by the tender grass and my hunger, that I could not resist nibbling a bit of it. I had no right to do it, I admit—'

A great uproar among the beasts interrupted him. Here was the culprit who had brought misfortune on all of them! What a horrible crime it was to eat grass that belonged to someone else! It was enough to hang anyone for, much more an Ass.

Immediately they all fell upon him, the Wolf in the lead, and soon had made an end to him, sacrificing him to the gods then and there, and without the formality of an altar.

The weak are made to suffer for
the misdeeds of the powerful.

Fable 35

The Bundle of Sticks

A certain Father had a family of Sons, who were forever quarreling among themselves. No words he could say did the least good, so he cast about in his mind for some very striking example that should make them see that discord would lead them to misfortune.

One day when the quarreling had been much more violent than usual and each of the Sons was moping in a surly manner, he asked one of them to bring him a bundle of sticks. Then handing the bundle to each of his Sons in turn he told them to try to break it. But although each one tried his best, none was able to do so.

The Father then untied the bundle and gave the sticks to his Sons to break one by one. This they did very easily.

'My Sons,' said the Father, 'do you not see how certain

it is that if you agree with each other and help each other, it will be impossible for your enemies to injure you? But if you are divided among yourselves, you will be no stronger than a single stick in that bundle.'

In unity is strength.

Fable 36

The Fir-Tree and the Bramble

A Fir-Tree said boastingly to the Bramble, 'You are useful for nothing at all; while I am everywhere used for roofs and houses.' The Bramble answered: 'You poor creature, if you would only call to mind the axes and saws which are about to hew you down, you would have reason to wish that you had grown up a Bramble, not a Fir-Tree.'

Better poverty without care, than riches with.

Fable 37

A Raven and a Swan

A Raven, which you know is black as coal, was envious of the Swan, because her feathers were as white as the purest snow. The foolish bird got the idea that if he lived like the Swan, swimming and diving all day long and eating the weeds and plants that grow in the water, his feathers would turn white like the Swan's.

So he left his home in the woods and fields and flew down to live on the lakes and in the marshes. But though he washed and washed all day long, almost drowning himself at it, his feathers remained as black as ever. And as the water weeds he ate did not agree with him, he got thinner and thinner, and at last he died.

A change of habits will not alter nature.

Fable 38

The Dog and His Reflection

A Dog, to whom the butcher had thrown a bone, was hurrying home with his prize as fast as he could go. As he crossed a narrow footbridge, he happened to look down and saw himself reflected in the quiet water as if in a mirror. But the greedy Dog thought he saw a real Dog carrying a bone much bigger than his own.

If he had stopped to think he would have known better. But instead of thinking, he dropped his bone and sprang at the Dog in the river, only to find himself swimming for dear life to reach the shore. At last he managed to scramble out, and as he stood sadly thinking about the good bone he had lost, he realized what a stupid Dog he had been.

It is very foolish to be greedy.

Fable 39

The Lioness

A controversy prevailed among the beasts of the field as to which of the animals deserved the most credit for producing the greatest number of whelps at a birth. They rushed clamorously into the presence of the Lioness and demanded of her the settlement of the dispute. 'And you,' they said, 'how many sons have you at a birth?' The Lioness laughed at them, and said: 'Why! I have only one; but that one is altogether a thoroughbred Lion.'

The value is in the worth, not in the number.

Fable 40
The Astrologer

A man who lived a long time ago believed that he could read the future in the stars. He called himself an Astrologer, and spent his time at night gazing at the sky.

One evening he was walking along the open road outside the village. His eyes were fixed on the stars. He thought he saw there that the end of the world was at hand, when all at once, down he went into a hole full of mud and water.

There he stood up to his ears, in the muddy water, and madly clawing at the slippery sides of the hole in his effort to climb out.

His cries for help soon brought the villagers running. As they pulled him out of the mud, one of them said:

'You pretend to read the future in the stars, and yet you fail to see what is at your feet! This may teach you to pay more attention to what is right in front of you, and let the future take care of itself.'

'What use is it,' said another, 'to read the stars, when you can't see what's right here on the earth?"

*Take care of the little things and the big
things will take care of themselves.*

Fable 41

The Thief and the Innkeeper

A Thief hired a room in a tavern and stayed a while in the hope of stealing something which should enable him to pay his reckoning. When he had waited some days in vain, he saw the Innkeeper dressed in a new and handsome coat and sitting before his door.

The Thief sat down beside him and talked with him. As the conversation began to flag, the Thief yawned terribly and at the same time howled like a wolf.

The Innkeeper said, 'Why do you howl so fearfully?'

'I will tell you,' said the Thief, 'but first let me ask you to hold my clothes, or I shall tear them to pieces. I know not, sir, when I got this habit of yawning, nor whether these attacks of howling were inflicted on me as a judgement for my crimes, or for any other cause; but this I do know, that when I yawn for the third time, I actually turn into a wolf and attack men.' With this speech he commenced a second fit of yawning and again howled like a wolf, as he had at first.

The Innkeeper, hearing his tale and believing what he said, became greatly alarmed and, rising from his seat, attempted to run away.

The Thief laid hold of his coat and entreated him to stop, saying, 'Pray wait, sir, and hold my clothes, or I shall tear them to pieces in my fury, when I turn into a wolf.' At the same moment he yawned the third time and set up a terrible howl.

The Innkeeper, frightened lest he should be attacked, left his new coat in the Thief's hand and ran as fast as he could into the inn for safety. The Thief made off with the coat and did not return again to the inn.

Every tale is not to be believed.

Fable 42

The Ass and the Lap Dog

There was once an Ass whose Master also owned a Lap Dog. This Dog was a favourite and received many a pat and kind word from his Master, as well as choice bits from his plate. Every day the Dog would run to meet the Master, frisking playfully about and leaping up to lick his hands and face.

All this the Ass saw with much discontent. Though he was well fed, he had much work to do; besides, the Master hardly ever took any notice of him.

Now the jealous Ass got it into his silly head that all he had to do to win his Master's favour was to act like the Dog. So one day he left his stable and clattered eagerly into the house.

Finding his Master seated at the dinner table, he kicked

The Ass and the Lap Dog

up his heels and, with a loud bray, pranced giddily around the table, upsetting it as he did so. Then he planted his forefeet on his Master's knees and rolled out his tongue to lick the Master's face, as he had seen the Dog do. But his weight upset the chair, and Ass and man rolled over together in the pile of broken dishes from the table.

The Master was much alarmed at the strange behavior of the Ass, and calling for help, soon attracted the attention of the servants. When they saw the danger the Master was in from the clumsy beast, they set upon the Ass and drove him with kicks and blows back to the stable. There they left him to mourn the foolishness that had brought him nothing but a sound beating.

Behaviour that is regarded as agreeable in one is very rude and impertinent in another.

Do not try to gain favour by acting in a way that is contrary to your own nature and character.

Fable 43
The Milkmaid and Her Pail

A Milkmaid had been out to milk the cows and was returning from the field with the shining milk pail balanced nicely on her head. As she walked along, her pretty head was busy with plans for the days to come.

'This good, rich milk,' she mused, 'will give me plenty of cream to churn. The butter I make I will take to market, and with the money I get for it I will buy a lot of eggs for hatching. How nice it will be when they are all hatched and the yard is full of fine young chicks. Then when May day comes I will sell them, and with the money I'll buy a lovely new dress to wear to the fair. All the young men will look at me. They will come and try to woo me—but I shall very quickly send them about their business!"

As she thought of how she would settle that matter, she

The Milkmaid and Her Pail

tossed her head scornfully, and down fell the pail of milk to the ground. And all the milk flowed out, and with it vanished butter and eggs and chicks and new dress and all the milkmaid's pride.

Do not count your chickens before they are hatched.

Fable 44
The Huntsman and the Fisherman

A Huntsman, returning with his dogs from the field, fell in by chance with a Fisherman who was bringing home a basket well-laden with fish. The Huntsman wished to have the fish, and their owner experienced an equal longing for the contents of the game-bag. They quickly agreed to exchange the produce of their day's sport. Each was so well pleased with his bargain that they made for some time the same exchange day after day. Finally a neighbour said to them, 'If you go on in this way, you will soon destroy by frequent use the pleasure of your exchange, and each will again wish to retain the fruits of his own sport.'

Abstain and enjoy.

Fable 45

The Gnat and the Bull

A Gnat flew over the meadow with much buzzing for so small a creature and settled on the tip of one of the horns of a Bull. After he had rested a short time, he made ready to fly away. But before he left he begged the Bull's pardon for having used his horn for a resting place.

'You must be very glad to have me go now,' he said.

'It's all the same to me,' replied the Bull. 'I did not even know you were there.'

We are often of greater importance in our own eyes than in the eyes of our neighbour.

The smaller the mind the greater the conceit.

Fable 46

The Miser

Miser had buried his gold in a secret place in his garden. Every day he went to the spot, dug up the treasure and counted it piece by piece to make sure it was all there. He made so many trips that a Thief, who had been observing him, guessed what it was the Miser had hidden, and one night quietly dug up the treasure and made off with it.

When the Miser discovered his loss, he was overcome with grief and despair. He groaned and cried and tore his hair.

A passerby heard his cries and asked what had happened. 'My gold! O my gold!' cried the Miser, wildly, 'someone has robbed me!"

'Your gold! There in that hole? Why did you put it there? Why did you not keep it in the house where you could easily get it when you had to buy things?"

The Miser

'Buy!' screamed the Miser angrily. 'Why, I never touched the gold. I couldn't think of spending any of it.'

The stranger picked up a large stone and threw it into the hole.

'If that is the case,' he said, 'cover up that stone. It is worth just as much to you as the treasure you lost!"

A possession is worth no more than the use we make of it.

Fable 47

The Cat, the Cock and the Young Mouse

A very young Mouse, who had never seen anything of the world, almost came to grief the very first time he ventured out. And this is the story he told his mother about his adventures.

'I was strolling along very peaceably when, just as I turned the corner into the next yard, I saw two strange creatures. One of them had a very kind and gracious look, but the other was the most fearful monster you can imagine. You should have seen him.

'On top of his head and in front of his neck hung pieces of raw red meat. He walked about restlessly, tearing up the ground with his toes, and beating his arms savagely against his sides. The moment he caught sight of me he opened his pointed mouth as if to swallow me, and then he let out a piercing roar that frightened me almost to death.'

Can you guess who it was that our young Mouse was trying to describe to his mother? It was nobody but the Barnyard Cock and the first one the little Mouse had ever seen.

'If it had not been for that terrible monster,' the Mouse went on, 'I should have made the acquaintance of the pretty creature, who looked so good and gentle. He had thick, velvety fur, a meek face, and a look that was very modest, though his eyes were bright and shining. As he looked at me he waved his fine long tail and smiled.

'I am sure he was just about to speak to me when the monster I have told you about let out a screaming yell, and I ran for my life.'

'My son,' said the Mother Mouse, 'that gentle creature you saw was none other than the Cat. Under his kindly appearance, he bears a grudge against every one of us. The other was nothing but a bird who wouldn't harm you in the least. As for the Cat, he eats us. So be thankful, my child, that you escaped with your life, and, as long as you live, never judge people by their looks.'

Do not trust alone to outward appearances.

Fable 48

The Monkey and the Dolphin

It happened once upon a time that a certain Greek ship bound for Athens was wrecked off the coast close to Piraeus, the port of Athens. Had it not been for the Dolphins, who at that time were very friendly towards mankind and especially towards Athenians, all would have perished. But the Dolphins took the shipwrecked people on their backs and swam with them to shore.

Now it was the custom among the Greeks to take their pet monkeys and dogs with them whenever they went on a voyage. So when one of the Dolphins saw a Monkey struggling in the water, he thought it was a man, and made the Monkey climb up on his back. Then off he swam with him towards the shore.

The Monkey and the Dolphin

The Monkey sat up, grave and dignified, on the Dolphin's back.

'You are a citizen of illustrious Athens, are you not?' asked the Dolphin politely.

'Yes,' answered the Monkey, proudly. 'My family is one of the noblest in the city.'

'Indeed,' said the Dolphin. 'Then of course you often visit Piraeus.'

'Yes, yes,' replied the Monkey. 'Indeed, I do. I am with him constantly. Piraeus is my very best friend.'

This answer took the Dolphin by surprise, and, turning his head, he now saw what it was he was carrying. Without more ado, he dived and left the foolish Monkey to take care of himself, while he swam off in search of some human being to save.

One falsehood leads to another.

Fable 49

The Cock and the Fox

One bright evening as the sun was sinking on a glorious world a wise old Cock flew into a tree to roost. Before he composed himself to rest, he flapped his wings three times and crowed loudly. But just as he was about to put his head under his wing, his beady eyes caught a flash of red and a glimpse of a long pointed nose, and there just below him stood Master Fox.

'Have you heard the wonderful news?' cried the Fox in a very joyful and excited manner.

'What news?' asked the Cock very calmly. But he had a queer, fluttery feeling inside him, for, you know, he was very much afraid of the Fox.

'Your family and mine and all other animals have agreed to forget their differences and live in peace and friendship

The Cock and the Fox

from now on forever. Just think of it! I simply cannot wait to embrace you! Do come down, dear friend, and let us celebrate the joyful event.'

'How grand!' said the Cock. 'I certainly am delighted at the news.' But he spoke in an absent way, and stretching up on tiptoes, seemed to be looking at something afar off.

'What is it you see?' asked the Fox a little anxiously. 'Why, it looks to me like a couple of Dogs coming this way. They must have heard the good news and—"

But the Fox did not wait to hear more. Off he started on a run.

'Wait,' cried the Cock. 'Why do you run? The Dogs are friends of yours now!"

'Yes,' answered the Fox. 'But they might not have heard the news. Besides, I have a very important errand that I had almost forgotten about.'

The Cock smiled as he buried his head in his feathers and went to sleep, for he had succeeded in outwitting a very crafty enemy.

The trickster is easily tricked.

Fable 50

The Old Woman and the Wine-Jar

An Old Woman found an empty jar which had lately been full of prime old wine and which still retained the fragrant smell of its former contents. She greedily placed it several times to her nose, and drawing it backwards and forwards said, 'O most delicious! How nice must the Wine itself have been, when it leaves behind in the very vessel which contained it so sweet a perfume!"

The memory of a good deed lives.

Fable 51

The Stag at the Pool

A Stag overpowered by heat came to a spring to drink. Seeing his own shadow reflected in the water, he greatly admired the size and variety of his horns, but felt angry with himself for having such slender and weak feet. While he was thus contemplating himself, a Lion appeared at the pool and crouched to spring upon him. The Stag immediately took to flight, and exerting his utmost speed, as long as the plain was smooth and open kept himself easily at a safe distance from the Lion. But entering a wood he became entangled by his horns, and the Lion quickly came up to him and caught him. When too late, he thus reproached himself:

'Woe is me! How I have deceived myself! These feet which would have saved me I despised, and I gloried in these antlers which have proved my destruction.'

What is most truly valuable is often underrated.

Acknowledgements

This completed work is a synergistic product of many minds.

I thank my husband, Rishi Sehgal, my entire family and all my dear friends for being patient and encouraging.

I bear a deep sense of sincere appreciation for Yamini Chowdhury for her efficient and professional approach to the work. My earnest regards to Aditi Mehrotra for devoting her valuable time and giving editorial inputs, which has helped shape this book. I express my gratitude to the most diligent team of Rupa Publications for their efforts.

To acknowledge is to express my gratitude to all of you who undoubtedly remain an integral part of my extraordinary journey. Your unwavering support and encouragement have truly made this book possible.